SAILOR JACK
AND THE
BALL GAME

by Selma and Jack Wassermann

pictures by William Lackey

Benefic Press   Chicago

Publishing Division of Beckley-Cardy Company
Atlanta   Dallas   Long Beach   Portland

CONTENTS

Copyright 1962 by Benefic Press

All Rights Reserved

Printed in the United States of America

Library of Congress
Number 62-10083

Ball Game Tomorrow

Sailor Jack works on the SHARK.

The SHARK is an atomic submarine.

Bluebell is the sailors' friend.

She plays with the sailors.

The sailors like Bluebell.

One day Bluebell got something.
It was something from Beanpole.
Beanpole was Jack's friend.
He worked on the SHARK, too.

"Now Bluebell can go with us
to the ball game tomorrow,"
said Beanpole.

"Ball game!" said Bluebell.
"Ding-ding!"

The SHARK's men were to
play ball.

They were to play with
the men of the WHIP.

The game was in Eastport.

They were going there now.

"Eastport! Eastport!"
a sailor said.

"There is Catfish Island,"
said Jack.

"And there is the lighthouse,"
said Beanpole.

To Eastport, went the
atomic submarine.

"Look!" said Beanpole.

"There is the WHIP!"

"And there is Bill Keen,"
said Jack.

"He works on the WHIP."

Beanpole laughed.

"He is your friend now.

But he will not be your
friend tomorrow," he said.

"No," said Jack.

"Tomorrow he will play with
the men from the WHIP.

He will be the WHIP's friend."

Jack and Beanpole looked at
the WHIP.

"Here come the men of the
WHIP now," said Beanpole.

The two sailors went to see
the WHIP's men.

Bluebell went, too.

"It is good to
see you, Jack!"
said Bill Keen.
"And it will be
good to win that
ball game from
you tomorrow!"
Jack and
Beanpole did not
like that.
"Is that so?"
said Beanpole.

Where Is Bluebell?

"We will win!" said Bill Keen.

"No, Bill," said Jack.

"Bluebell will be at the
game tomorrow.

When Bluebell is with us,
we win!"

"We win!" said Bluebell.

"Is that so?" said Bill Keen.

He looked at Bluebell.

Bluebell did not like
what Bill said.

"Aaaaaak!" she said.

Bill laughed.

"We will see!" he said.

"We must go back to the SHARK
and sleep now," said Beanpole.

"Sleep will not help you win
the game tomorrow!" said Bill.

"Bluebell will help us win!"
Jack said.

Then they all said good night.

Jack, Beanpole, and Bluebell
went back to the SHARK.

"Bill Keen is
up to something!"
said Jack.
"I know,"
Beanpole said.
"But what?"
"Aaaaaak!"
said Bluebell.

The sailors went to sleep.
In the night some one came.

Then the day came.
It was the day of the game.

"I do not see Bluebell,"
said Beanpole.

"Where can she be?"
said Jack.

Then he said, "Bluebell?"
Bluebell did not come.

"Where is she?"
said Beanpole.

"She is not
here!" said Jack.

21

"Did you see Bluebell?" Jack
said to the other sailors.

"We will help you look,"
said the sailors.

But no one saw Bluebell.

"Bill Keen
knows we must
have Bluebell to
win that game!"
said Jack.

"With Bluebell
there, we are
happy," said
Beanpole.

"She helps win!"
"Bill and the
WHIP's men must
have come for
Bluebell in the
night," said
Jack.

Looking For Bluebell

"We will go to see the captain," said Jack.

Captain White was the captain of the submarine.

"What is it?" said the captain.

"The WHIP's men have Bluebell," said Jack.

"Now we can not win the ball game," said Beanpole.

"Go out there and find her!" said Captain White.

Jack and Beanpole went back
to the other sailors.

"We must find Bluebell,"
they said.

"The captain said we must
all help look."

The SHARK's men went to work.

Some looked
in Eastport.

Some looked
on other boats.

Jack went to see Bill Keen.

"What did you do with
Bluebell?" said Jack.

Bill Keen laughed.

"I have not seen her!" said Bill.

Jack went back to the SHARK.

All the men went back to the
SHARK.

"We can not find Bluebell,"
they said.

"What will we do now?" said
Beanpole.

"It will soon be time for
the ball game."

"Is there some where we did not look?" said Jack.

"Did we look in the lighthouse?" said Beanpole.

"No!" said a sailor.

"There is not time," Jack said.

"We must go to the game with out Bluebell."

Then a sailor said,
"Look! Look!
There is something
on Catfish Island!"

Jack looked.

"That is Bluebell!" he said.

"And there is a man from the WHIP with her!"

"So now we know where Bluebell is," said Beanpole.

"But it is time for the game. We can not go for her now."

To Catfish Island

"You and the others go on to the game," said Jack to Beanpole.

"I will go for Bluebell in the little boat.

When I can, I will come to the game with her."

Jack got in to the little boat.

He went fast.

Soon he came to Catfish Island.

Jack got out of the boat.

"I must look out now," he said.
"No one must know I have come."

There were
two ways to go.
He did not
know what way
to go.
"Now what?"
he said.
Then he saw
something.

"This is Bluebell's!" said Jack.
"That must be the way to go!"
And that was the way he went.
He went fast now.

There was the lighthouse!

There, too, was one of the

WHIP's men.

But the sailor was sleeping.

Jack did not see Bluebell.

"She must be in there,"

he said.

Little by little, Jack went on.
He came up to the sailor.
The sailor went on sleeping.
Jack looked in.
There was Bluebell.

"Shhhhhh!" said Jack.
"Shhhhhh!" said Bluebell.
She jumped on Jack.
The sailor went on sleeping.
Little by little, Jack and
Bluebell went by the sleeping
sailor.

"Shhhhhh!" said Jack again.

"Shhhhhh!"
said Bluebell.
But then she
said, "Ding-ding!"
That did it!

Up jumped the
WHIP sailor!
He came fast!
Jack and
Bluebell ran.
They ran
and ran.

41

Soon they came to the boat.
In to the boat, they jumped.
Then Jack looked.
The WHIP's man was running.
But he had no boat!
"Now you will see us win
that game!" Jack said.

Jack worked fast.

"We must get to the ball game," said Jack.

Then they came to Eastport.

They ran and ran.

Bluebell At The Game

When the SHARK's men saw Jack
and Bluebell, they were happy.
"Here is Bluebell!" they said.

"Are we winning?" said Jack.

"No," Beanpole said.

"We did not hit the ball.

They hit the ball two times.

But now you and Bluebell

will help us win."

"Come on, Beanpole,"
a sailor said.
"You are up now."
The ball came.
Beanpole looked.
But the ball went by.

Again the ball came.
Beanpole tried to hit it.
The ball went by again.

Captain White
tried.

He did not
hit it.

Things did not
look good.

Then Jack went up.

He had worked in the boat.

He had run and run
to the game.

Jack did not hit the ball.

Then Jack did
something good!
The ball came
to Jack.
Jack hit it!

"Look at that, Bluebell,"
said Beanpole.

"Jack hit the ball.

But we must hit the ball
again to win.

You must help us."

"Aaaaaak!" said Bluebell.

Soon the WHIP
men went up.
A WHIP man
tried to hit
the ball.

The ball went
past him.
The ball went
to Bluebell!

The ball came at Bluebell!
Bluebell saw it come.
Up she jumped!
"Aaaaaak! Aaaaaak!"
she said.

"Look at Bluebell!"
a sailor said.

"Go get her, Jack!"
said Captain White.

"We can not have her up there!"
Jack ran to Bluebell.

"Come here, Bluebell!"
said Jack.

"This is no way to help us win
the game!"

But Bluebell did not come.

"Aaaaaak!" she said.

Jack jumped to get her.

Bluebell went up.
Jack went up, too.

When he came back he had
Bluebell.

"Come on, Bluebell!"
he said.

"I can see this is not
your day for helping!"

A WHIP man was up.
He tried to hit the ball.
He hit the ball!

The ball went to Captain White.
He tried to get the ball.
It went on by.

Jack was back of the captain.
He got the ball!
The WHIP man was out!

It was time for the SHARK men
to play.

Beanpole went up.

"Come on, Beanpole," said
Jack.

"Come on, Beanpole," said
Bluebell.

The ball came at Beanpole.
He looked at the ball.
Then he tried to hit it.
He did!
Then he ran.

Soon it was time
for Jack.
"Come on,"
said Bluebell.
"Come on!
Ding-ding!"

When the ball
came, Jack hit it.
Up! Up!
Up went the ball.

"What a hit!" said a man.

"Run, Jack," a SHARK man said.

"Run, run!" said Bluebell.

Jack ran.

He ran fast.

"A home run!" said Captain White.

"We won!" said a SHARK sailor.

"Bluebell helped us win!"
said Jack.

"We win!" said Bluebell.

And all the SHARK men laughed.

Vocabulary

The total number of words in this book is 106. Of these, 7 are first-grade words and appear below in roman type; 7 are above first-grade level and appear below in italic type. The numbers indicate the pages on which each word first appears.

The remaining 92 words are below first-grade level and have not been listed on this page.

atomic 5	game 7	*sailors* 5
		submarine 5
	hit 45	
boats 27		
	lighthouse 9	tomorrow 7
captain 24		tried 47
	man 8	
friend 6	other 22	*win* 11